Good-Bye Tonsils!

JULIANA LEE HATKOFF AND CRAIG HATKOFF

ILLUSTRATED BY MARILYN METS

VIKING

To all children who have to go to the hospital
—J.H.

To my niece without tonsils —Jenny!
—M.M.

VIKING
Published by the Penguin Group
Penguin Putnam Books for Young Readers, 345 Hudson Street, New York, New York 10014, U.S.A.
Penguin Books Ltd, 27 Wrights Lane, London W8 5TZ, England
Penguin Books Australia Ltd, Ringwood, Victoria, Australia
Penguin Books Canada Ltd, 10 Alcorn Avenue, Toronto, Ontario, Canada M4V 3B2
Penguin Books (N.Z.) Ltd, 182-190 Wairau Road, Auckland 10, New Zealand
Penguin Books Ltd, Registered Offices: Harmondsworth, Middlesex, England

First published in 2001 by Viking, a division of Penguin Putnam Books for Young Readers.

1 3 5 7 9 10 8 6 4 2

Text copyright © Juliana and Craig Hatkoff, 2001
Illustrations copyright © Marilyn Mets, 2001
All rights reserved

LIBRARY OF CONGRESS CATALOGING-IN-PUBLICATION DATA
Hatkoff, Juliana.
Good-bye tonsils! / by Juliana Hatkoff and Craig Hatkoff; illustrated
by Marilyn Mets.
p.   cm.
Summary: A young girl describes what happens when she goes to the
hospital to have her tonsils removed.
ISBN 0-670-89775-2 (hardcover)
[1. Tonsillectomy—Fiction. 2. Hospitals—Fiction.] I. Hatkoff,
Craig. II. Mets, Marilyn, ill. III. Title.
PZ7.H28445 Go 2001 [E]—dc21 00-010694

Printed in Hong Kong
Set in Excelsior

A Note to Parents

Twenty years ago, over a million pediatric tonsillectomies were performed annually. Today, despite powerful new antibiotics, over 250,000 tonsillectomies are still performed each year in the United States, the majority on an outpatient basis. It is of critical importance to prepare children well for a tonsillectomy or other surgical procedure in order to avoid unnecessary trauma.

Here are some basic guidelines:

- Children should meet the surgeon and, if possible, visit the hospital in advance of the operation.
- Be honest with your child and explain clearly why this is being done, what is going to happen, and how they will feel afterwards.
- Assure them you will be there when they go to sleep and when they wake up. Parents are now encouraged to accompany their child into the operating room.
- Have your child explain back to you what they think will happen, in order to clear up any misconceptions. Keeping a journal together is an excellent collaborative way to mitigate anxieties.
- Be reassuring, but don't tell them they should not be scared.
- Let them bring a soothing toy or possession along with them.
- Be positive. Parents must be informed, confident, and in charge.

We both agree that a book to help children who are to undergo surgery, and their families, is long overdue. *Hurray Juliana!*

DR. ROBERT F. WARD
New York Otolaryngology Institute
Associate Professor of Otolaryngology
Weill Medical College of Cornell University

HAROLD S. KOPLEWICZ M.D.
Director, Child Study Center
Arnold and Debbie Simon Professor of Child and Adolescent Psychiatry
New York University School of Medicine

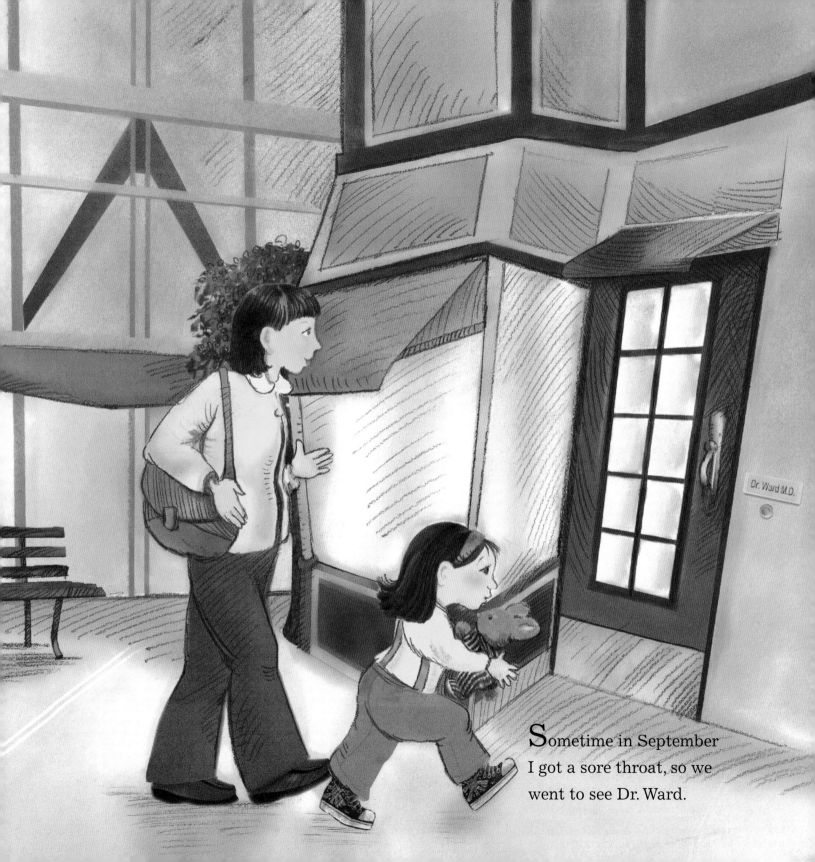

Sometime in September
I got a sore throat, so we
went to see Dr. Ward.

"Say aahh," said Dr. Ward. Then he said, "In the last twelve months Juliana has had five throat infections that we've had to treat with antibiotics. And you say she has been complaining frequently that her throat is bothering her. Sounds to me like her tonsils may have to come out. Let's see how she does over the next few weeks."

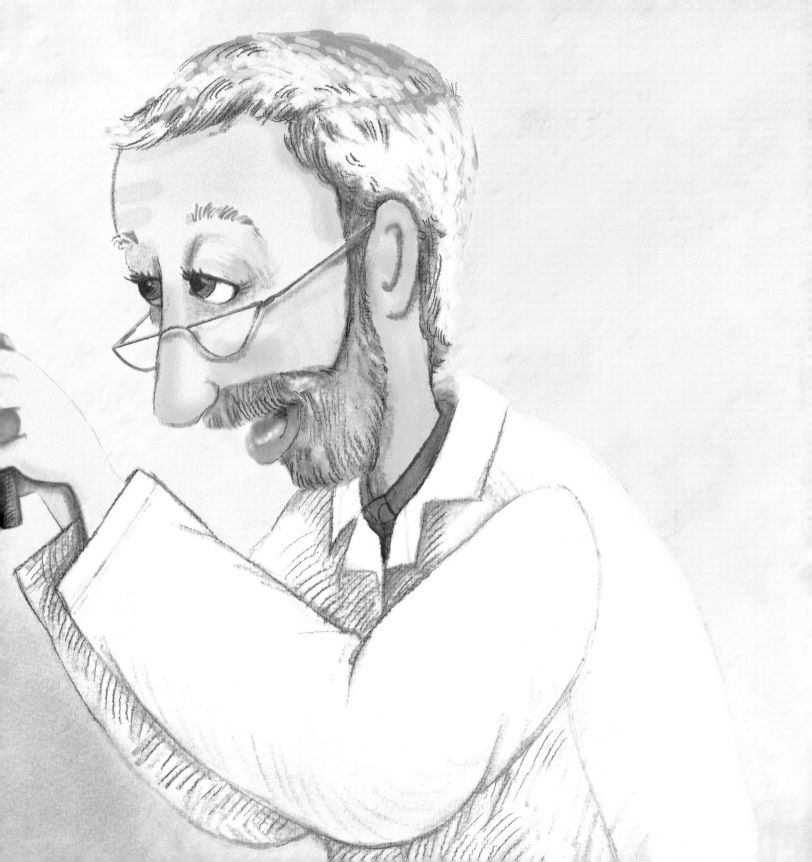

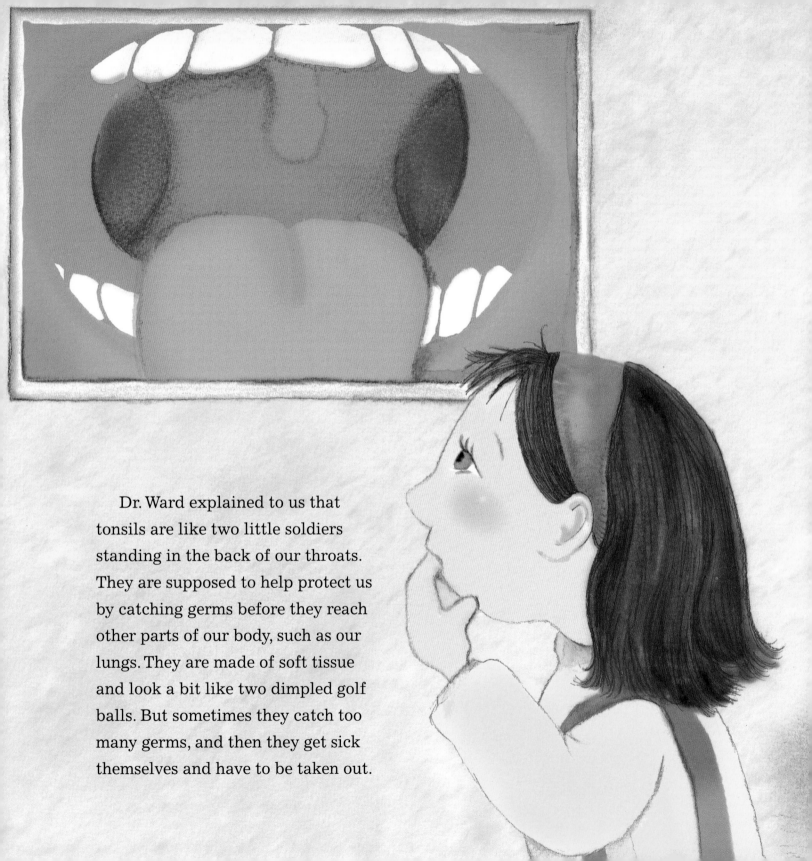

Dr. Ward explained to us that tonsils are like two little soldiers standing in the back of our throats. They are supposed to help protect us by catching germs before they reach other parts of our body, such as our lungs. They are made of soft tissue and look a bit like two dimpled golf balls. But sometimes they catch too many germs, and then they get sick themselves and have to be taken out.

In October my throat still hurt. We went back to see Dr. Ward again. He told us that the only way to make my throat feel better was to take out my tonsils. This meant that I would have to go to the hospital and have an operation. Sometimes kids have to stay overnight in the hospital, but I wouldn't. I could have the operation and come home the same day.

Dr. Ward explained that I would be asleep and wouldn't feel anything during the operation. When I woke up my throat would feel sore and it would be hard to swallow for a couple of days. But he said I would also get to eat all the ice cream I wanted. Even though I love ice cream, I was scared.

We did a few things that made me feel better about having my tonsils out.

I read the *Curious George* book about when he swallows a wooden puzzle piece and has to go to the hospital. I also re-read the *Madeline* book where she has her appendix out, and all her classmates want their appendixes out too when they discover you get presents.

What really helped me most was talking to my friend Storey, who has had three operations. Storey had to stay in the hospital for a couple of days after each operation. She told me about the "magic mask with the magic gas" that you put over your mouth to make you go to sleep. I thought she was really brave. We bought special blue masks at the drugstore and wore them when we played hospital.

She told me that you sleep in beds that can go up and down or make you sit up or make your feet higher than your head. She told me that she got to wear a special nightgown with teddy bears on it. After her operations when she had to go to the bathroom, she went in a special metal bowl called a bedpan, because she was supposed to stay in bed for a whole day.

Thursday, October 14, around 5:00 P.M. Tomorrow is my operation and it is also my sister Isabella's first birthday. Since I may not feel so great after my operation tomorrow, Mommy and Daddy gave a little party for both of us today. We had two cakes. One was for Isabella's birthday, and one was a special cake for me that said, GOOD-BYE TONSILS. We also got some presents. I was nervous about going to the hospital, but the cake cheered me up.

Finally it was Friday, October 15, the day of the operation.

6:30 A.M. It was time to go to the hospital. I was still nervous and I even cried. I couldn't have anything to eat that morning. I was very thirsty when I woke up, so my daddy gave me a little apple juice around 5:00 A.M. My mommy thought I should wear my pajamas to the hospital, but I didn't want to, so I wore my "comfy clothes." I packed a few books and a couple of toys, and I brought my blanket with me. We got to the hospital around 7:00 and went to the big admissions desk. We had to fill in lots of papers. The people at the desk gave me a blue plastic bracelet that had my name on it. They asked me to check the spelling of my name—Juliana. They had spelled it right. Then they put the bracelet around my ankle. I was still a little scared.

Then around 7:45 A.M. it was time to change into a special nightgown that had little elephants on it. I remembered that Storey told me hers had bears but I liked the elephants. They also gave me slipper socks. I sat in a big chair with my mommy, and then the nurse took a picture of me with my mommy and daddy. Dr. Ward came in to see how I was, and he introduced me to a different doctor who would put the magic mask over my mouth that would make me go to sleep. Dr. Ward told me the other doctor was called an anesthesiologist, and that it is a hard word to say.

Around 8:00 A.M. Dr. Ward told me that soon the nurse would ask me to drink some red cherry-flavored liquid from a little plastic cup. He said this would make me feel good, and I might even feel a little silly. After the nurse gave me the liquid, I started to feel a little sleepy, and I wasn't scared or nervous anymore.

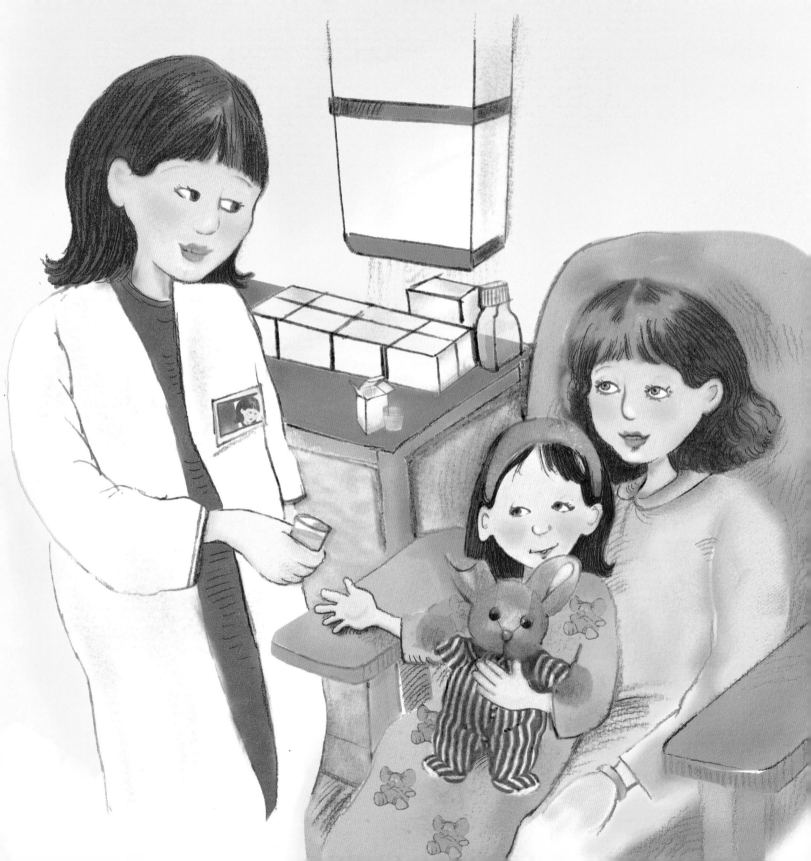

Around 8:30 A.M. I was feeling very relaxed, and the nurse told my mommy to hold on to me tightly so I wouldn't slip or fall. My mommy and daddy put on special gowns and these funny paper slippers. Then my mommy carried me into the operating room. I was very sleepy. Dr. Ward strapped me carefully onto the operating table so I wouldn't fall off. Dr. Ward was wearing a little blue paper mask that covered his mouth and nose, just like the ones Storey and I had played with. The anesthesiologist was also wearing a little blue mask. She showed me the magic mask that was made of clear plastic and told me that I should breathe deeply as she put the magic mask over my mouth. My mommy and daddy each kissed me and told me how much they loved me. And that's all I remember about the operation.

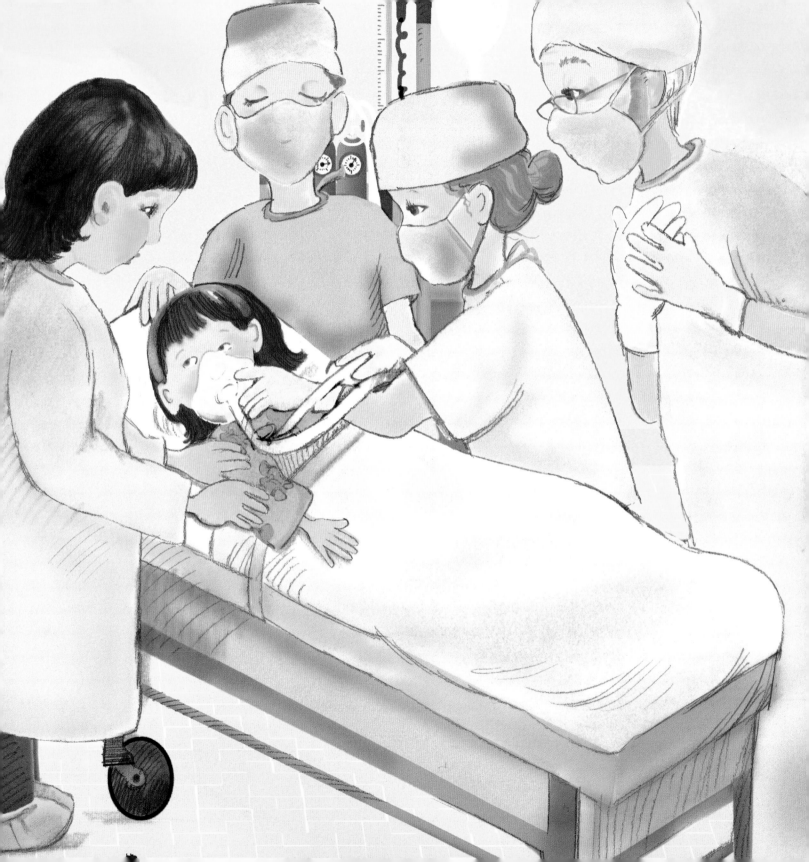

By 9:30 A.M. the operation was over. The next thing I remember is waking up in the recovery room. I was in a bed and my mommy was with me. I felt funny and my throat hurt every time I swallowed, but it wasn't too bad. There was a little needle in my wrist that didn't hurt. I didn't really like having it, but I knew I couldn't take it out. It is called an IV and it feeds liquid to your body. You need it because they don't let you eat or drink before your operation or right after it. Even though you may not feel like eating or drinking, your body is thirsty and needs liquid. It really is nothing to worry about because you can't even feel it.

A little boy named Matthew was sitting in a big chair nearby. Dr. Ward had taken his tonsils out just before mine. Soon I moved over to a chair right across from Matthew. We talked to each other a lot, although we both sounded funny. I was glad Matthew was there.

By noon Matthew was ready to go home. I was sad to see him leave, but they told me if I slept a little I could go home soon too. I closed my eyes for a few minutes and the next thing I knew . . .

It was 12:30 P.M. and it was time for me to go home.

My daddy came into the recovery room. He had brought me a Popsicle. Now it was time to get dressed. In the cab on the way home the medicine they gave me wore off, and my throat really hurt for a few minutes. Daddy dropped Mommy and me off and went to get medicine for the pain, but he also bought all kinds of ice cream, Popsicles, and ice-cream sandwiches. I took some medicine that I didn't like to take, but then I ate lots of ice cream and slept on and off for the rest of the day. I also opened some presents. My favorite was a snow-cone maker I got from my friend Jack and his sisters. The snow cones didn't taste very good, but they were fun to make.

On Saturday, October 16, I watched cartoons and movies and kept falling asleep.

My throat was very sore and scratchy. I coughed a couple of times, and that really hurt, but just for a second or two. Because it hurt to swallow, I didn't like taking my medicine, even though I knew it would make me feel better. I tried to swallow as little as possible. It was pretty funny, because my mouth would fill up with saliva and I was drooling everywhere. My mommy and daddy made me hold a kitchen towel under my chin. We all laughed, because I looked pretty silly.

Sunday was another big ice-cream day.

I had a lot of company—my grandmother, aunts and uncles and cousins all came to visit. It was fun to see everyone, and I wanted to tell them all about my tonsils, but it was still a little hard to talk. That's when my daddy said that maybe I should write a book about it.

Monday, October 18. I felt fine and I wanted to go to school. It was raining out, and my mommy wanted me to stay home one more day. I cried because she wouldn't let me go to school. I wanted to tell all my friends about my tonsils. But I got pretty tired, so it was probably good that I stayed home. When my throat hurt I thought about something else or had a little ice cream, and it stopped hurting. I usually only get to chew gum once in a while, but Dr. Ward said chewing gum was very good for helping my throat heal, so I got to chew lots of gum. My daddy told me not to get too used to chewing it.

Tuesday, October 19. Today I went back to school. I was very excited, and I told my whole class all about my operation. I told them about the presents, all the ice cream you could eat, that the doctor made me chew gum, and that it really didn't hurt very much. I told them that even though I had been scared, there was really nothing to be scared about. In fact, the worst thing about having your tonsils out is . . .

. . . you can only do it once!